Dear Willie Rudd,

Dear Willie Rudd,

By Libba Moore Gray
Pictures by Peter M. Fiore

ALADDIN PAPERBACKS

New York   London   Toronto   Sydney   Singapore

First Aladdin Paperbacks edition January 2000

Aladdin Paperbacks
An imprint of Simon & Schuster Children's Publishing Division
1230 Avenue of the Americas
New York, NY 10020

The Library of Congress has cataloged the hardcover edition as follows:
Gray, Libba Moore. Dear Willie Rudd, / by Libba Moore Gray ;
illustrated by Peter M. Fiore.   p.   cm.
Summary: An adult remembers her childhood relationship with a black woman
and wishes she could thank her and apologize for any wrongs committed due to race.
ISBN 0-671-79774-3 (hc.)
[1. Race relations—Fiction.   2. Afro-Americans—Fiction.]
I. Fiore, Peter, ill.   II. Title.   PZ7.G7793De   1993
[E]—dc20   92-25064   CIP
ISBN 0-689-83105-6 (ISBN-13: 978-0-689-83105-6) (pbk.)

For Nancy and Robbie,
Myra and Jeff Daniel,
and for Cathy—
extraordinary teachers all.

L.M.G.

For my children,
Lisa and Paul

P.M.F.

Miss Elizabeth felt troubled. She went out on the front porch and sat in her grandmother's big, green wicker rocker. And she rocked, and she rocked, and she rocked.

She put her head back and closed her eyes. She could smell the perfume from the blossoms on the tall magnolia tree in the side yard. She could hear the bees buzzing...buzzing around the abelia bushes in the front yard. She could hear the mourning doves, the color of evening, cooing in the backyard. And Miss Elizabeth remembered. She remembered all the way back fifty years when she was a very little girl.

She remembered Willie Rudd, now surely gone
to heaven if anyone ever has.

She remembered the feel of Willie's big lap, covered
with a flowered apron, the feel of Willie's generous
bosom against her cheek.

She remembered Willie's songs, rumbling up through
her large body and out her mouth:

> Hush. Hush. Somebody callin' my name.
> Hush. Hush. Somebody callin' my name.
> Come up my chile on my right hand
> and look and see de Promised Land.
> Hush. Hush. Oh, yes.
> Somebody callin' my name!

She remembered her wearing leather shoes, split on the sides to comfort those feet that used to give her such miseries.

She remembered her on her knees, scrubbing the patterned linoleum floor.

Miss Elizabeth opened her eyes.
She stood up.
She went into the house and got her pen
and her best writing paper with the flowers
on the border.
Then she sat down and wrote:

Dear Willie Rudd,

I'm writing this letter for my mother and for my grandmother and for me.

I'm writing to say thank you. And I'm writing to say I'm sorry for anything any of us might have done to make you sad.

Most of all I'm writing to say I wish you could come to see me once again.

This time you would come in my front door...not my back door.

You would eat with me at our polished table on the good china…not in the kitchen alone.

We would go to the movies and sit together in the front row.

*We would ride the bus, and you would sit
in the front seat with me beside you.*

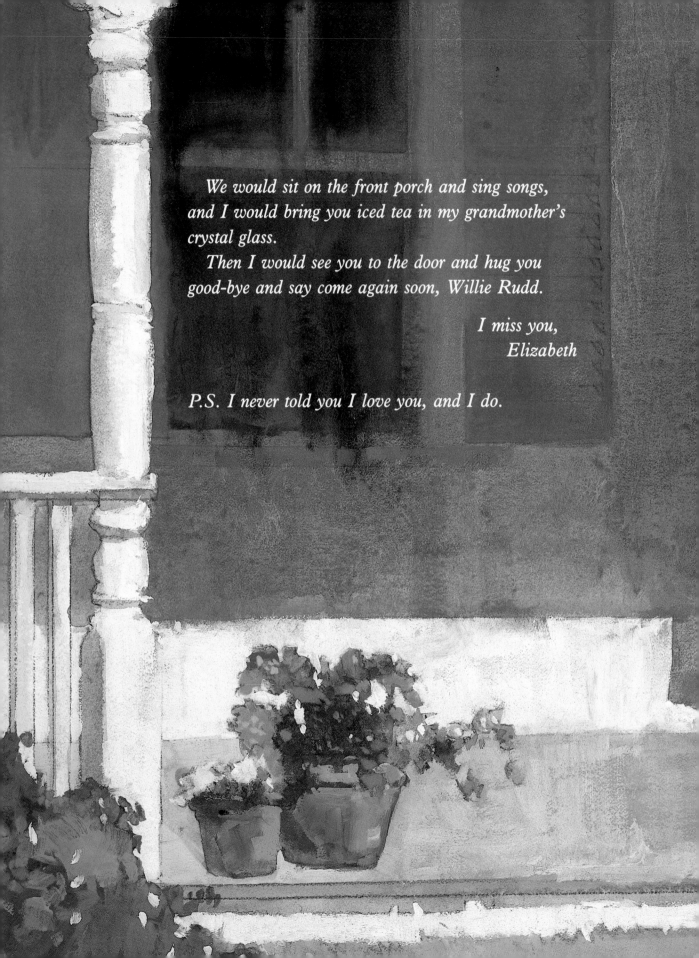

We would sit on the front porch and sing songs,
and I would bring you iced tea in my grandmother's
crystal glass.
  Then I would see you to the door and hug you
good-bye and say come again soon, Willie Rudd.

I miss you,
Elizabeth

P.S. I never told you I love you, and I do.

Then Miss Elizabeth folded the letter and tied it to a shiny red kite.

She walked slowly to the top of the hill, and when the wind had grown strong enough so that her gray hair blew back from her face, she let go of the kite, string and all.

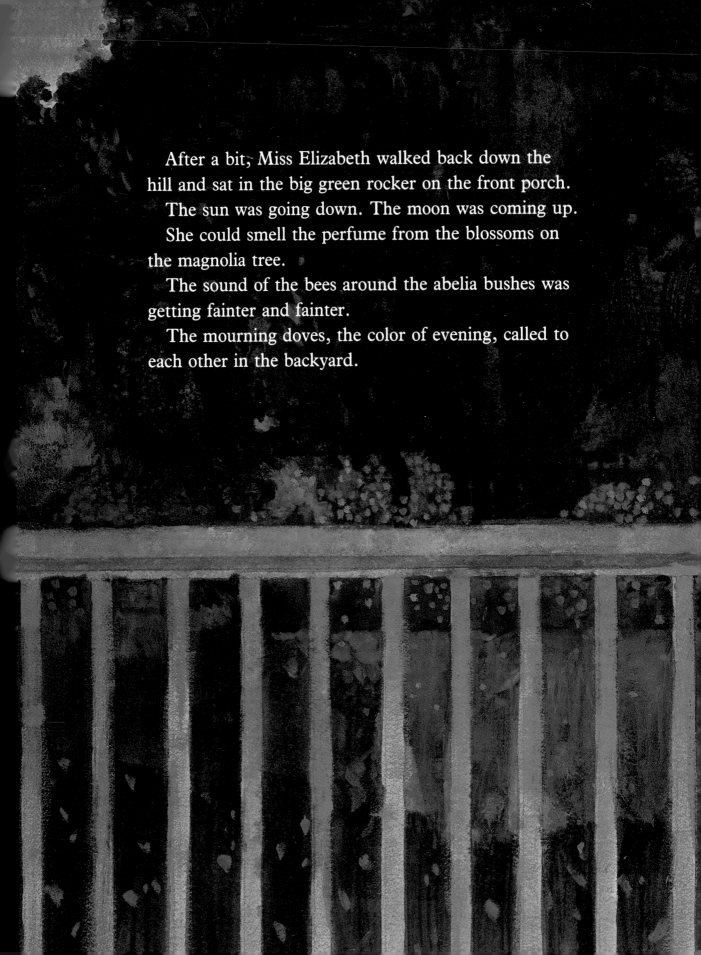

After a bit, Miss Elizabeth walked back down the
hill and sat in the big green rocker on the front porch.

The sun was going down. The moon was coming up.

She could smell the perfume from the blossoms on
the magnolia tree.

The sound of the bees around the abelia bushes was
getting fainter and fainter.

The mourning doves, the color of evening, called to
each other in the backyard.